DOLPHIN

D

DELPHINIUM

EUCALYPTUS

E

ERMINE

FOX

F

FOXGLOVE

JAY

J

JASMINE

KIWIFRUIT

K

KIWI

LIZARD

L

LILAC

POPPY

P

PENGUIN

QUETZAL

Q

QUINCE

ROSE

R

RABBIT

VIOLET

V

VOLE

WISTERIA

W

WHALE

XENICIDAE

X

XERANTHEMUM

ZEBRA

Z

ZUCCHINI

Mother Nature Nursery Rhymes

by Mother Nature

Illustrated by Itoko Maeno

Advocacy Press, Santa Barbara

For
Young Environmentalists
Everywhere

Text copyright © 1990 by Sandy Stryker and Mindy Bingham
Illustrations copyright © 1990 by Itoko Maeno

Special thanks to William P. Sheehan

All rights reserved. No part of this book may be reproduced in any form
without permission in writing from Advocacy Press, P.O. Box 236, Santa Barbara,
California 93102, USA, except by a newspaper or magazine reviewer who wishes
to quote brief passages in a review.

 Published by Advocacy Press
P.O. Box 236
Santa Barbara, CA 93102

Library of Congress Cataloging-in-Publication Data

Stryker, Sandy, 1945-
Bingham, Mindy, 1950-
Mother Nature Nursery Rhymes

I. Maeno, ill II. Title.

ISBN 0-911655-01-8

girls
inc. *Advocacy Press is a division of Girls Incorporated of Greater Santa Barbara,*
an affiliate of Girls Incorporated of America.

Editor and Art Director, Penelope C. Paine
Layout and typography, Christine Nolt

Printed in Hong Kong

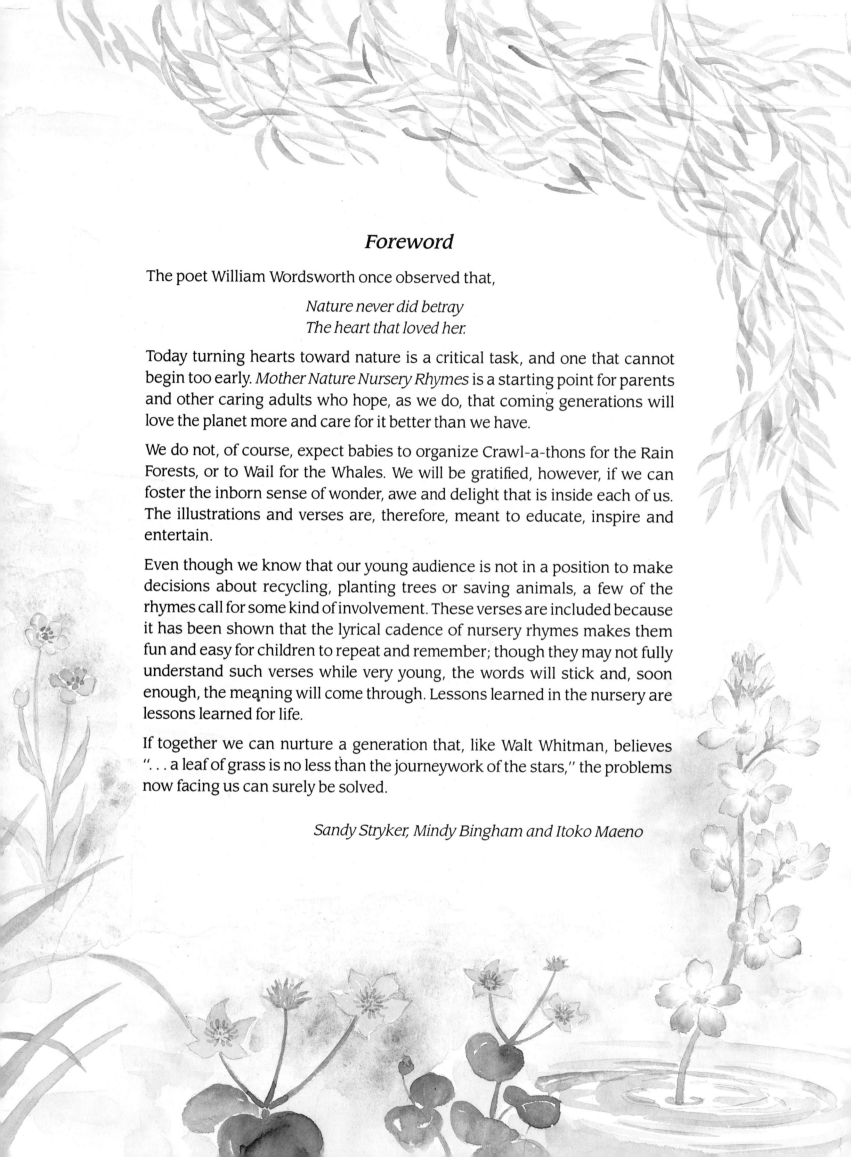

Foreword

The poet William Wordsworth once observed that,

Nature never did betray
The heart that loved her.

Today turning hearts toward nature is a critical task, and one that cannot begin too early. *Mother Nature Nursery Rhymes* is a starting point for parents and other caring adults who hope, as we do, that coming generations will love the planet more and care for it better than we have.

We do not, of course, expect babies to organize Crawl-a-thons for the Rain Forests, or to Wail for the Whales. We will be gratified, however, if we can foster the inborn sense of wonder, awe and delight that is inside each of us. The illustrations and verses are, therefore, meant to educate, inspire and entertain.

Even though we know that our young audience is not in a position to make decisions about recycling, planting trees or saving animals, a few of the rhymes call for some kind of involvement. These verses are included because it has been shown that the lyrical cadence of nursery rhymes makes them fun and easy for children to repeat and remember; though they may not fully understand such verses while very young, the words will stick and, soon enough, the meaning will come through. Lessons learned in the nursery are lessons learned for life.

If together we can nurture a generation that, like Walt Whitman, believes "...a leaf of grass is no less than the journeywork of the stars," the problems now facing us can surely be solved.

Sandy Stryker, Mindy Bingham and Itoko Maeno

In Tune with Mother Nature

If you listen for the songbirds
As they greet the summer sun,
And love the way the wind can make
The trees sing just for fun;

If you like to hear the ocean
As it drums upon the shore,
And imagine all the whales out there,
And hope they'll sing some more;

If you think of all the animals
As players in a band,
Each with a lovely tune to play,
All needed on the land;

And know that as a boy or girl
A woman or a man
You have a vital role to play
In Mother Nature's plan;

If you honor every living thing
As a part of nature's treasure
You're in tune with Mother Nature
So let's all sing her song together.

What an Otter Ought to Do

Have you ever thought of
What an otter ought to do,
Instead of playing water sports
And having fun like you?

Ought an otter be a farmer?
Ought an otter go to school?
Ought an otter be an auditor,
Or join the typing pool?

How odd to be an otter
If an otter had to run
To catch a bus or hop a train.
Maybe otters just ought to have fun!

What Is a Rainbow?

A rainbow is what happens
When the raindrops break up light
If the sun is still behind you,
But the rain is in your sight.

This bridge of every color
Is a wonder to behold.
When nature gives such treasure,
Who needs a pot of gold?

Everyday Is Earth Day

Everyday is Earth Day,
If it's cold or wet or hot
Pitch in to save the planet
It's the only one we've got.

Why Does Thunder Follow Lightning?

Why does thunder follow lightning,
Not the other way around?
Why don't we hear the thunder clap,
Then see light strike the ground?

Though the two start out together,
Lightning always wins the race.
Sound tries hard to go as fast,
But it's light that sets the pace.

Five Little Penguin Chicks

Five little penguin chicks, all in a row,
Dressed up for dinner with no place to go.
"Oh!" they imagine, "What wonder! How nice,
Something to eat besides raw fish on ice!"

Ride a Quick Horse

Ride a quick horse
To Willow Creek Cross
To see the wild mustangs
Before they are lost.

Without our protection
They might disappear.
What a sad fate
For this brave pioneer.

Water

Water's what we bathe in,
Water's what we drink.
Water's what keeps plants alive.
Without it, fish would sink.

Water comes from rivers,
Water comcs from rain,
And every drop that's wasted
Is just water down the drain!

Mother Nature

Mother Nature's
Very wise
She makes the laws for
Earth and skies.

Presidents and Queens,
And Kings
Must dance when
Mother Nature sings.

Mary, Mary Quite Contrary

Mary, Mary quite contrary
How does your garden grow?
With scarecrows and marigolds
and onions all in a row.

Two Mighty Condors

Two mighty condors perched in a tree.
One named Mallory, the other named Lee.

Fly away Mallory, fly away Lee.
Come back condors . . . now there are three!

To Market, to Market

To market, to market
Let's take our string bag.
Home again, home again
Ziggety zag.

Plastic and Glass

Plastic and glass
Plastic and glass
Recycle these items
Don't put in the trash.

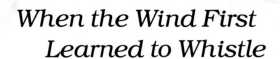

When the Wind First Learned to Whistle

When the wind first learned to whistle,
It went off to show the trees.
"That must be hard," a tall oak said.
The wind said, "It's a breeze!"

Some Daddies Are Mommies

Some daddies are mommies,
The seahorse, for one;
He holds all the eggs in his pouch.
After twelve days, he gives birth to the young.
Clearly, this dad is no slouch.

The male Darwin's frog
Is another fine dad.
When given the eggs, he just swallows.
The eggs turn to tadpoles and frogs form from tads
That are spat out til dad's sack is hollow.

Some water bug dads,
Have eggs glued to their backs
Parenting's something they share.
These dads do their duties both gladly and well
For a baby's a family affair!

Northern Lights

The northern lights may move and crack
As though the sky were breaking.
But never fear, it's just an act
Of Mother Nature's making.

When arcs of light fill up the night
Like dancers at a palace,
Just sit back. Enjoy the show:
Aurora borealis.

Flying Fish and Dancing Bees

Flying fish and dancing bees,
What acrobats compare with these?
Bees dance to show their friends the way
To nectar, near or far away.
But why do fishes leap about?
To spread their wings, without a doubt.

The King of Beasts

Though the lion is the king of beasts,
He's quite a funny cat.
He doesn't purr, stays out of trees,
And wears a big fur hat.

He roars instead of meowing,
He likes to take a swim.
What's more, he weighs five hundred pounds.
My kitty's not like him.

Dragonflies and Fireflies

On a misty moisty morning
In the middle of July,
We walk along the water's edge
To seek the dragonflies.

On a sultry summer's evening
It's the fireflies we see,
A million tiny light bulbs
Burning bright for you and me.

What Would Mother Nature Do?

What would Mother Nature think
Of trees burned down and air that stinks?
With dirty water in her sink,
What would Mother Nature think?

What would Mother Nature say
Of creatures who have gone away —
The kinds once here that aren't today?
What would Mother Nature say?

What would Mother Nature do
To make the planet clean anew?
If she was standing here with you,
What would Mother Nature do?

Raccoons

When it comes to table manners
Some animals are rude.
Raccoons, though, are quite proper,
They even wash their food.

15

Ten Little Elephants

One little, two little, three little elephants
Four little, five little, six little elephants
Seven little, eight little, nine little elephants
Ten little elephants play.

Ten little, nine little, eight little elephants
Seven little, six little, five little elephants
Four little, three little, two little elephants
Just one little elephant left.

Ladybug, Ladybug

Ladybug, ladybug
Fly away home
Your garden's in trouble
No more should you roam.

The aphids are munching,
The leafhoppers hop.
We don't want to spray them
So please make them stop.

Hey Diddle Diddle

Hey diddle diddle
It's not wise to fiddle
With Mother Nature's grand design.

There's room for us all
So let's answer her call
For our lives are all intertwined.

If . . .

If mouses are mice,
And louses are lice,
And gooses are geese,
Are two mooses, meese?

Save the Pandas

Round and round the world
To save the pandas everywhere
One stop, two stop
Tickle me under there.

19

Waterbird, Shorebird

Waterbird, waterbird
In the lagoon
Shorebird, shorebird
On the sand dune.

Sandpiper, pelican
Cormorant, coot
Kingfisher, heron
Ruddy Duck, loon.

Ology, Ology

Ology, ology, microbiology
ecology, geology, too.
Ology, ology, meteorology
biology, zoology, zoo.

Sing a Song of Sixpence

Sing a song of sixpence
Paper full of dyes
Four and twenty fishes
Pay with their lives.

Wouldn't it be better
If our paper goods were plain.
We shouldn't want them colored
If it causes so much pain.

Dinosaurs

Stegosaurus, kronosaurus,
Tyrannosaurus rex;
Dinosaurs were all once tinct,
But now they are all ex.

Triceratops, iguanodon,
And diplodocus, too;
How much we miss these creatures
That we never even knew.

The Pollution Solution

The pollution solution has only two parts.
Just look around and you'll see.
What has eight limbs and four eyes and two brains?
That's right? It's you and it's me!

23

The Rap on Garbage

Too much garbage,
Not enough space.
Got to be careful
Not to replace
Tulips with tin cans,
Meadows with glass,
Forests with dump grounds,
Fresh air with gas.
Reuse or recycle,
Don't throw things away.
Let's make a new start here,
Begin a new day.
From the depths of the ocean
To the top of the Alps,
Every litter bit hurts,
Every little bit helps.

Hedgehogs

Eating bugs in the garden at night
The hedgehog's a most welcome sight.
He ruffles and snuffles
And then off he shuffles
To sleep in a ball rolled up tight.

Plant a Tree and Grow a Home

Plant a tree and grow a home.
It's quite a lovely deal.
Few other forms of housing
Are as decorative or real.

There are badgers in the basement,
And insects down below;
While up above are butterflies
And bees and squirrels and so.

Way up in the penthouse,
All sorts of birds are nesting
As ivy climbs around the trunk
And long-eared bats are resting.

A tree, you see, is much more
Than leaves upon some logs —
It's a living condominium
One of nature's vital cogs.

It's a Magical World

It's a magical world,
Mother Nature's domain,
With millions of wonders to see,
And to hear and to smell,
And to taste and to touch;
So many fine places to be!

Without Mother Nature
There wouldn't be grass,
Or puddles, or mud good for squishing.
There wouldn't be sunshine,
Or icy cold lakes
On the day that you want to go fishing.

Every stone on the beach
And shell on the shore
Is evidence of her attention;
To toe-tickling artwork
Right there at your feet,
Treasures too many to mention.

Mother Nature plants flowers
And oversees trees
And cares about each living creature.
Remember her words
And learn of her ways.
Mother Nature's an excellent teacher.

It's Up to People

It's up to people to save all the trees
That still find a home in our woods.
Animals don't wield the power we do,
Though they'd certainly help if they could.

We'd see warthogs and pigs
To save fiddleleaf figs;
Baby chicks cheeping
To keep willows weeping;
Cats with a shine
For the loblolly pine;
Polars and pandas
To save jacarandas;
Even queen bees and princesses
For photosynthesis.

But it's up to people to save all the trees
That still find a home in our woods.
Animals don't wield the power we do,
Though they'd certainly help if they could.

The Giving Grace

Bees give us honey,
Worms give us silk,
Birds give us music,
Cows give us milk.

Trees give us shelter,
Flowers, perfume.
Sheep provide wool
We can weave on a loom.

Geese give us feathers,
Chickens give eggs.
Horses give rides
Flying fast on fine legs.

Dogs give us friendship,
Cats bring us joy.
We can give thanks —
Every girl and each boy.

Bedtime Prayer

Now I lay me down to sleep,
Please help me learn my world to keep;
To guard the air and skies of blue,
The oceans, lakes and rivers too;
Save the mighty forest lands,
The plains, the shores and desert sands,
Protect all creatures wild and free
In air, on land and in the sea.

Lullaby

Rock-a-bye, baby,
In the tree top.
When the wind blows,
Your cradle will rock.

Birds serenade you,
Stars guard the night.
Slumber in peace
'Til morning brings light.

Passed down from generation to generation and shared by many cultures, activity rhymes are favorites with children. Reinforcing the words, the actions make rhymes more fun and, therefore, more memorable. Activity rhymes encourage hand-eye coordination which is a vital step in a child's learning process, and they provide parents and caregivers with a source of instant amusement.

The following rhymes can be accompanied by hand actions:

Page 6

Ride a Quick Horse

Recite this version of the traditional Mother Goose rhyme while gently bouncing your child on your knee; or, with crossed legs, using one ankle as a saddle, swing your leg up and down.

Page 8

Two Mighty Condors

For this rhyme place a little piece of moistened paper to each index fingernail and on one little fingernail.

Two mighty condors, perched in a tree.
Wiggle the index fingers representing each bird.

One named Mallory,
Wiggle one index finger.

The other named Lee.
Wiggle the other index finger.

Fly away Mallory,
Tuck one index finger into your palm.

Fly away Lee.
Do the same with the other hand

Come back Condors, now there are three!
Bring back both index fingers and the one little finger wiggling.

This may also be played by hiding your hands behind your back.

Page 13

Ten Little Elephants

For this finger-counting game, raise the corresponding number of fingers as you recite the rhyme.

Page 15

Save the Pandas

Round and round the world
To save the pandas everywhere
With your index finger, tickle a circle on the palm of your child's outstretched hand.

One stop,
Make a step with your finger to the forearm and touch.

Two stop,
Touch the inside of the elbow

Tickle me under there.
Tickle under the chin.

This version of the classic *Round and Round the Garden* rhyme permits the introduction of the role of zoos in the preservation of a vanishing species. The panda's natural habitat is found only in the Himalayas and northern China.

Page 17

Ology, Ology

This is like the Pat-a-Cake game.
Facing each other, slap your thighs, clap your hands together, and then pat against each other's hands at eye level.

Ology, Ology, microbiology
 Slap   Clap   Pat   (pause)

Ecology, geology, too
 Slap   Clap   Pat   (pause) and so on.

For a variation, pat each other's opposite hands for the second and third line.

Here are some other activities you might like to share:

Mother Nature is all around us. See if your child can find her in each of Itoko Maeno's beautiful illustrations.

Learn Mother Nature's alphabet as illustrated on the end sheets.

Sing new words to old tunes for *Sing a Song of Sixpence, Ride a Quick Horse, Mary, Mary Quite Contrary,* and *Lullaby (Rock-a-bye, Baby)*. Make up your own tune for our new rhymes.

"If (children) are to keep alive their inborn sense of wonder . . . (they) need the companionship of at least one adult who can share it, rediscovering with (them) the joy, excitement and mystery of the world we live in."

— Rachel Carson, author of *Silent Spring*
and environmental pioneer

Beginning in the nursery, children's values and perceptions are most strongly influenced by the words and actions of their parents or other primary caregivers. That is why the nursery rhymes, word games and ditties learned in early childhood have such a powerful impact. Add to this the sing-song quality and repetitive nature of the rhymes and it is easy to see why children will carry the words with them throughout their lives.

If we hope to raise a generation of ecologically sound adults, we must follow Rachel Carson's advice and take time to be both the mentor and teacher. **Mother Nature Nursery Rhymes** can help instill a strong love of nature in even the youngest child. Reinforcing the messages with simple, but appropriate, actions will further increase their impact.

Here are a number of things you can do:

Let your child help you plant and tend a garden that includes natural pest controls such as marigolds, onions and ladybugs. Together, create a scarecrow with old clothes, hats, twigs and straw.

With older children discuss the plight of endangered species such as the panda, the condor, the elephant and the mustang. Ask the questions "What is currently being done to save these animals?" "Can you think of other appropriate solutions to the problems?"

Support local, state and national environmental groups. Many have excellent magazines, newsletters and programs for children.

Demystify the language of science. It is known that toddlers have a greater ability to learn words than they will at any other time in their life. Teach rhymes such as *Ology, Ology* and *Dinosaurs* with the same language expectations as any simpler rhyme.

Help your children be more aware of nature by renewing your own acquaintance with the physical world. Take time to smell the flowers, listen to the birds or watch the fireflies. Teach your child to use all his or her senses — sight, touch, hearing, smell and taste.

Impress upon children that there should be no biases based on gender, race, nationality or religion. All of creation should be treated with love and respect.

Decorate your child's room with pictures of plants, animals and other natural phenomena. When you share a rhyme or story about one of these natural wonders, ask the child to identify it on his or her wall.

When shopping, choose uncolored or unbleached paper goods to set an example for children in the family. Remember to use your own string bag or basket whenever possible.

Check television guides for nature shows and watch them with your child. Borrow nature oriented videos from your local library.

Visit your local natural history museum, botanical gardens, zoological gardens or science museum.

Even very young children can help recycle plastic, glass, aluminum and paper. As you hand them an item to be placed in the proper bin, you might recite *Plastic and Glass* together.

Make environmental concerns an intergenerational activity. Because great-grandparents and grandparents lived in times of greater scarcity, ask them to share the conservation efforts they learned as children and how "things" were recycled, saved and valued?

Imagine what the world could be like, if when today's children become tomorrow's decision-makers they remember to ask the question, *"What would Mother Nature do?"*

Index

Books by Advocacy Press

Choices: A Teen Woman's Journal for Self-awareness and Personal Planning, by Mindy Bingham, Judy Edmondson and Sandy Stryker. Softcover, 240 pages. ISBN 0-911655-22-0. $16.95.

Challenges: A Young Man's Journal for Self-awareness and Personal Planning, by Bingham, Edmondson and Stryker. Softcover, 240 pages. ISBN 0-911655-24-7. $16.95.

More Choices: A Strategic Planning Guide for Mixing Career and Family, by Mindy Bingham and Sandy Stryker. Softcover, 240 pages. ISBN 0-911655-40-9. $15.95.

Changes: A Woman's Journal for Self-awareness and Personal Planning, by Mindy Bingham, Sandy Stryker and Judy Edmondson. Softcover, 240 pages. ISBN 0-911655-40-9. $16.95.

Mother-Daughter Choices: A Handbook for the Coordinator, by Mindy Bingham, Lari Quinn and William Sheehan. Softcover, 144 pages. ISBN 0-911655-44-1. $7.95.

Women Helping Girls with Choices, by Mindy Bingham and Sandy Stryker. Softcover, 192 pages. ISBN 0-911655-00-X. $9.95.

Minou, written by Mindy Bingham, illustrated by Itoko Maeno. Hardcover with dust jacket, 64 pages with full-color illustrations throughout. ISBN 0-911655-36-0. $14.95.

My Way Sally, by Mindy Bingham and Penelope Paine, illustrated Itoko Maeno. Hardcover with dust jacket, 48 pages with full-color illustrations throughout. ISBN 0-911655-27-1. $14.95.

Father Gander Nursery Rhymes: The Equal Rhymes Amendment, by Father Gander. Hardcover with dust jacket, full-color illustrations throughout. ISBN 0-911655-12-3. $14.95.

Tonia the Tree, by Sandy Stryker, illustrations by Itoko Maeno. Hardcover with dust jacket, 32 pages with full-color illustrations throughout. ISBN 0-911655-16-6. $13.95.

Kylie's Song, by Patty Sheehan, illustrated by Itoko Maeno. Hardcover with dust jacket, 32 pages with full-color illustrations throughout. ISBN 0-911655-19-0. $13.95.

Berta Benz and the Motorwagen, written by Mindy Bingham, illustrated by Itoko Maeno. Hardcover with dust jacket, 48 pages with full-color illustrations throughout. ISBN 0-911655-38-7. $14.95.

Time for Horatio, written by Penelope Paine, illustrated by Itoko Maeno. Hardcover with dust jacket, 48 pages with full-color illustrations throughout. ISBN 0-911655-33-6. $14.95.

Mother Nature Nursery Rhymes, written by Mother Nature, illustrated by Itoko Maeno. Hardcover with dust jacket, 32 pages with full-color illustrations throughout. ISBN 0-911655-01-8. $14.95.

You can find these books at better bookstores. Or you may order them directly by sending a check for the amount shown above (California residents add appropriate sales tax), plus $3.00 each for shipping and handling, to Advocacy Press, P.O. Box 236, Dept. MN, Santa Barbara, California 93102. For your review, we will be happy to send you more information on these publications. Proceeds from the sale of these books will benefit and contribute to the further development of programs for girls and young women.